A Bottle of Happiness

Pippa Goodhart
Ehsan Abdollahi

There was once a **big mountain**.

The people on one side of the mountain
caught fish and mined jewels and grew crops.

They were rich, and they worked
hard at getting richer. They had a
big market where they sold things
to each other.

The people on
the other side of the mountain
worked hard too, but their soil was poor,
so crops grew less well. They had no sea to fish in
or jewels to mine. They grew and made just enough for
them all to eat and wear if they shared things. Because they
lived together, they loved sharing stories too. They told the same
stories over and over again.

But, one day, a child called Pim said,
"I want to find a new story. I'm going over
the mountain to see what's on the other side."

So Pim and Tiddle the dog climbed right up
to the top of the mountain. Then they looked
down and saw …

"Wow, look at that, Tiddle!"
said Pim.

Pim and Tiddle ran down to
the market. There was more
there than Pim had
known even existed in
the whole world!

Pim asked a stallholder,
"Please may I eat one of those beautiful fruits?"
"What will you give me in return for the fruit?"
said the man.
"I haven't got anything," said Pim.
"There must be something that your people
have that we don't," said a woman.
Pim looked at the market people.

"I think we have more happiness than you do,"
said Pim. "Bring us some of that, then,"
said the man.

So Pim walked back over the mountain, thinking about how to carry happiness.
I'll catch some laughter, thought Pim.
"Uncle Froddie, please will you sing for us?" said Pim.

Uncle Froddie sang and Tiddle danced. People laughed. Pim carefully caught
laughter in a bottle. Some music and love slipped in with it.

Pim put the stopper into the bottle to stop the happiness from leaking out.

Then Pim
and Tiddle ran
with the bottle
of happiness back
over the mountain.
It was light to
carry.

"Here's some happiness," said Pim, offering the bottle.

"Open it up," said the woman.

"I need to see how good your happiness is
before I know how many fruits to
exchange for it." "It's really good,"
said Pim. "It's got laughing
and music and love in it."

Pim pulled the stopper
from the bottle. Pim
tipped the bottle
to pour out the
happiness,
but what
came
out
was
...

... *silence*

and nothing to see.

"What a
silly child to think that
you could bottle laughter and
love and music!" scoffed the man. But,
"Listen properly!" said Pim. Because now
there was laughter! It was bursting and bubbling
and spreading from person to person.
They were laughing at Pim for
thinking that you could catch
happiness in a bottle.
"You said there was music, too,"said the man.
"I can't hear any of that.
I can't see the love either."
"Listen and look again,"
said Pim.

"Ha ha ha, ho, ho, hee,

Prance and dance and be happy!
Waggle your bum and stamp
your feet. Clap your hands
to mark the beat,"
sang Pim.

Soon everyone
was joining in
with the singing
and dancing and
laughing. When
Pim's song stopped,
they hugged each
other and laughed
some more.

After that, the market people shared their food and drink with Pim's people, and nobody weighed-up the weight of fruit against the weight of happiness. They just shared. The market people were amazed to see that Pim's people still had lots of happiness, even though they had given away a bottle of it.

And when everyone
was full of food and drink,
there was still a story to share.
Pim began the story,
"There was once a big mountain …"
And you know how that story goes on,
because you have shared it with
Pim and Tiddle already.

About this book

A new fable that goes full circle as it explores the value of possessions against values of friendship and fun. This story offers lots for children to think about and learn from, illustrated with jazzy patchwork pictures in a style that they might like to try out for themselves.

About the author

Pippa Goodhart is the author of over a hundred children's books, including prize-winning picture book *You Choose*, and the *Winnie the Witch* storybooks which she writes under the pen name of Laura Owen. She trained as a teacher, and worked for many years in bookselling before becoming and mother and a writer.

About the illustrator

Ehsan Abdollahi has worked as an illustrator of children's picture books as well as magazines and newspapers. He also makes animations and teaches illustrating in the university. He loves to create illustrations with watercolour. The illustrations of *A Bottle of Happiness* are in watercolour too. Ehsan says when he was working on this book he was living in the southern part of Iran (where he was born), and was inspired by the environment, fabrics and clothes of the people of that region to use sharp colours and rich patterns in his illustrations. Ehsan has also illustrated *When I Coloured in the World*, published by Tiny Owl.